GOOP
TALES
ALPHABETICALLY TOLD

Are you a Goop?

GOOP TALES

ALPHABETICALLY TOLD

A Study of the Behavior of some Fifty-two
Interesting Individuals, Each of Which
While Mainly Virtuous, yet has Some
One Human & Redeeming Fault;
With Numerous Illustrations

By GELETT BURGESS

DOVER PUBLICATIONS, INC.
NEW YORK

This Dover edition, first published in 1973, is an unbridged and unaltered republication of the work originally published by the Frederick A. Stokes Company in 1904.

International Standard Book Number: 0-486-22914-9
Library of Congress Catalog Card Number: 72-93766

Manufactured in the United States of America
Dover Publications, Inc.
180 Varick Street
New York, N.Y. 10014

GOOP
TALES
ALPHABETICALLY TOLD

TO
WILLIAM
HYDE IRWIN
FROM
FRANK
GELETT BURGESS

BOYS

CONTENTS

GIRLS

THE ETHEL—MR. JACK CYCLE

GOOP
TALES
ALPHABETICALLY TOLD

Are you a Goop?

INTRODUCTION

CHILDREN are human, I confess,
Though interesting none the less;
For often one redeeming fault
Is like the necessary salt
That brings a flavor rich and sweet
Into the viands that you eat.
But there are faults like pepper, too —
And like Tabasco not a few.
So, if you find you have a vice,
Be sure it's just the proper spice;
Of over-seasoning have a fear,
And use it only once a year!
Three hundred virtues to one vice
Will keep you reasonably nice. [teach,
That's what the Goops have come to
For they have only one of each!

This is the way Abednego acts when he is told to go to bed. He doubles up his fists, and says, "I won't!" Abednego and Haychu and Zeemsneaze were all out in the garden playing horse. Abednego's sister Ethel called to them to come into the house, for it was five o'clock. They all three ran in as fast as they could, for they thought that perhaps she had some candy for them. Zeemsneaze put his cap on the hall table, and his drum on the floor. They found that Mr. Jack, the young man who came so often to see Ethel, was in the drawing-room with her, and Henry, the butler, was just bringing in some tea and cakes for them. Abednego raised his hat very politely, and gave Ethel a pink he had picked in the garden. But when she told him it was time for him to go to bed, he threw his hat on the floor, and stamped his foot, and said, "I won't!" But Haychu obeyed promptly, and you can see she is half-way upstairs already, calling to Zeemsneaze. Abednego would not stir, so Mr. Jack had to carry him upstairs, saying,

"Some one told me that there were Goops in this house;

Are you a Goop?"

(2)

ABEDNEGO

ABEDNEGO would Raise his Hat,
And Bow, and Smile, and Things like That;
His Face and Hair were always Neat,
And when he Played he did not Cheat—
But Oh, the Awful Things he Said,
When it was Time to Go to Bed!

(This Goop is called ABEDNEGO because to bed he
would not go)

THIS picture shows what a Goop Bawlfred could be, when he wanted to. He was out doors, playing with Whymusty and Nibolene. Whymusty had on his soldier cap, and Nibolene was eating a doughnut as usual. After a while they heard a noise down the street, and saw an automobile coming along. It was Bawlfred's Uncle Harry, and on the back seats were Ethel and Miss Stilcum of Washington, who was visiting at the house. They had been riding in the Park. Whymusty said, "let's race them!" and so the three children started running as fast as they could. Whymusty was ahead, and Nibolene's hat had blown off, when Bawlfred stumbled and fell and hurt himself. But instead of getting up with a laugh, he began to cry! Just then his mother came along, and as she picked him up, she said,

"*Are you a Goop?*"

BAWLFRED

Young BAWLFRED took peculiar Pride
In Making Others Satisfied;
One Time I Asked him for his Head;
"Why, Certainly!" young Bawlfred said.
He was Too Generous, in Fact;
But Bravery he Wholly Lacked!

(This Goop is called BAWLFRED because he bawls
when he is hurt)

CAWLOMAR and Goblick and Carolesse were playing in the library when
Mother came into the room. She said she wanted to write a letter
to Father, and that the children must all go out into the stable to
play, where they could make all the noise they wanted to. So Cawlomar put his toys carefully away on the top shelf. First, his box of
building blocks, then his gas-ball and his funny wooden horse and
the flannel elephant. Then all three went out quietly. When they
got into the kitchen they found two loaves of chocolate cake Katy
the cook had just baked. Goblick and Carolesse each picked a piece
of frosting off and ate it, while Katy was not looking. Cawlomar
went right back into the library and told his mother what they had
done! She was very sorry about it, but sorrier that Cawlomar should

tell tales. "You shall all three be
punished for being so naughty," she
said. "Goblick and Carolesse must
stand in the corner for ten minutes
for being so greedy, and Cawlomar
must do the same for running and
telling on them!

Are you a Goop?"

(6)

CAWLOMAR

Of Tidy Children, CAWLOMAR
Was quite the Tidiest, by Far!
He always put his Toys Away
When he had Finished with his Play;
But Here his List of Virtues Ends—
A Tattle-Tale does Not Make Friends.

(This Goop is called CAWLOMAR because he always
calls his Ma and tells on his brothers and sisters)

It was a cloudy day when Mr. Jack called on Ethel, and, as they feared it might rain, they did not go out to walk, as they had intended, but stayed in the library. Mr. Jack is showing Ethel a card trick, and she is trying to find out how it is done. When it began to sprinkle, the Goops came into the house and began to watch Mr. Jack.

Askalotte, with her bell, is sitting by Ethel, but to-day she is behaving very well, and is quite still. Inkfinga has his bottle, as usual, and you can see how dirty his fingers are, but Ethel is so much interested in Mr. Jack that she does not notice how untidy that little Goop is, as he always behaves so nicely.

When Dowanto came in, Ethel asked him to put his kite away in the closet, and he scowled and said, "I don't want to!" When she told him to sit on a chair and watch Mr. Jack quietly, he said, "I don't want to!" When she said he must go up into the nursery, he cried and screamed, "I don't want to!"

Dowanto has just found a card on the floor; Ethel is asking him to give it to Mr. Jack, and Dowanto is saying, "I don't want to!"

Mr. Jack is very tired of hearing this ill-bred speech, but as he is very fond of Ethel, he does not say a word.

It ended by Ethel's having to stop and send all the Goops upstairs. Askalotte and Inkfinga went laughing, but Dowanto stamped his foot on the floor and cried, "I don't want to go!"

"O, Dowanto!" Ethel said,

"Are you a Goop?"

DOWANTO

DOWANTO, so his Parents said,
Just simply Loved to Go to Bed;
He was as Quiet as could Be
Whenever there were Folks to Tea;
But Still, he often had a Way
Of Grumbling, when he should Obey!

(This Goop is called DOWANTO because when his parents
ask him to do anything, he says "*I don't want to!*")

First, you must know the names of the people in this picture. The lady on the sofa is Miss Curleykew. Fibius is standing beside her. You need not be afraid that the spiders on the sofa will crawl over him, for they are really only buttons. The old gentleman in the cane-chair is Grandfather, who has fallen asleep while reading "David Grieve." You can see the book on his lap. In the very front is Elostum. He looks very much troubled because he has lost his cap and can't find it anywhere. When he came into the house he threw it on the floor. Teeza is behind him helping him look for it.

You see, Miss Curleykew has been telling them a story, and when she finished, she told them that they might go out into the woodshed and see the little kittens that came that morning. Elostum is very fond of animals and is in a great hurry, but he can't find his cap. Fibius is laughing at him, for *he* knows where it is. It is on the floor, under Grandfather's chair. You can just see one end of it.

Miss Curleykew said, " if you had hung it up properly, you 'd know where it is ! Goops *never* put their things away !

Are you a Goop? "

ELOSTUM

1 Fancy that ELOSTUM Knew
As Much as I, or even You!
He was Too Thoughtful, I am Sure,
To Soil or Scratch the Furniture;
Still, he was Careless, so They Say,
He Never Put his Things Away!

(This Goop is called ELOSTUM because whenever he
forgot to put his things away, he lost 'em)

Fɪʙɪᴜs and Lemeetri were out in the
barnyard playing horse. Of course Lemeetri had to be the driver first, or he would n't
play. So he took Fibius's whip, while Fibius
ran with Lemeetri's windmill. Then Fibius
said, "let's throw stones and see who can
come nearest to that window in the barn
without hitting it. Erlydyn came along just then, and she said,
"you'd better not do it, for you may break the window-pane!" But
the two Goops did try it, and after they had thrown a few stones, one
that Fibius threw went right through the glass.

Miss Curleykew, who had been pruning a rose bush, came running
up, when she heard the smash, and so did Cousin Billy, who had been
raking the lawn. "Who broke that window?" said Cousin Billy.
Nobody answered.

"Did you, Lemeetri?" Lemeetri answered, "no!"

"Did you do it, Erlydyn?" Erlydyn said, "no!"

Cousin Billy turned to Fibius and said, "did you do it, Fibius?"

Fibius said, "no, I did n't do it, Lemeetri did it with a stone!"

Then Miss Curleykew, who had seen it all, said, "O, Fibius, how
can you tell such a fib?

Are you a Goop?"

FIBIUS

The gentle FIBIUS Tried his Best
To Please his Friends with Merry Jest;
He Tried to Help them, when he Could,
For FIBIUS, he was Very Good;
As he was Good, I can't say Why
The gentle FIBIUS used to Lie!

(This Goop is called FIBIUS because he tells fibs)

WHEN the Goops' mother told them that Mr. Jimmy Payson was coming to dinner, they all wanted to be at the table, because he always made them laugh. But Korlaway annoyed her mother so much, and Obaynotte was so naughty that they were not allowed to eat dinner with the company. Only Goblick was permitted to sit at the table, and when they began dinner, what do you think he did?

He licked his fingers, he licked his knife, you never saw such a sight in your life! He growled at the food, and he kicked at his chair, he wiped off his spoon and his fork on his hair! He talked while he chewed, and he teased for more sauce, he took the best orange, and drank like a horse! He played with the salt, and he played with his food, his eating was horribly, horribly rude! He scraped at his plate, and he spilled all his soup, he sneezed and he coughed like the worst kind of Goop. He made such a mess with his butter and bread that his mother could stand it no longer, and said,

"Goblick, leave the table instantly. I never saw you behave so badly!" You see Obaynotte and Erlydyn watching him on the stairs? Erlydyn is calling out, "Goblick, Goblick, you make *me* sick!

Are you a Goop?"

GOBLICK

When GOBLICK was but Four Years Old
His Parents seldom had to Scold—
They seldom Called him "GOBLICK *don't!*"
He did not Scowl, and say, "*I won't!*"
Yet Now 'tis Sad to see him Dine—
His Table Manners are not Fine!

(This Goop is called GOBLICK because he gobbles his
food and licks his fingers)

HATESOPE disliked to take his bath so much that once he told Ethel he would strike her with his bat, if she got any soap in his eyes. I think he didn't really mean it, but he thought it was funny to say it. But he put off his bath as long as he could, and always made a shocking fuss over it. It always took him a long time to undress and place his clothes on a chair, hoping that Ethel would let him off from his washing. He is in the tub now, and is screaming that he is cold and that there is soap in his eyes, and anything else he can think of. It is Elostum's turn next, and he loves to take a bath, so he is all ready. He has taken his coat off, and come into the bathroom in his trousers, and is laughing at Hatesope. Gablia is talking as usual, waiting for her turn to come.

Ethel is hurrying as fast as she can, because she is going to the theatre with Mr. Jack, and she is saying, "if you'd only *not* squirm, Hatesope, it would be over more quickly!"

Gablia is saying, "I'm going to bring in my little ducks and fishes and put them in the water with me, and I hope it will take Ethel four hours to wash me!"

Elostum is saying, "Hatesope ought to have to eat a whole cake of soap to keep him from crying! Hatesope, why do you yell so?

Are you a Goop?"

HATESOPE

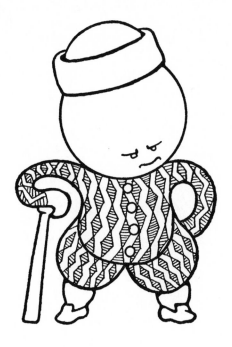

How Hale and Happy HATESOPE Seemed!
He never Nagged, he seldom Screamed;
His Company was Quite a Treat
To all the Children on the Street;
But Nurse has Told me of his Wrath
When he was Asked to Take a Bath!

(This Goop is called HATESOPE because he hates soap
and dislikes to be washed)

HERE you see Sister Ethel, and Mr. Jack is with
her, of course, for he comes to the house quite
often. This time he brought a lovely book called "The Confessions
of a Minor Poet," and Ethel laughed a great deal when she read it
and looked at the pictures. Then Mr. Jack began to read his diary
to her, and she forgot that there were any Goops in the room.

But Abednego and Ugpert were there playing their "doctor"
game. Abednego is the doctor, and when Ugpert comes in, he looks
at her tongue and feels her pulse. But they wouldn't let Inkfinga
play, because when he holds Ugpert's hand, he always leaves a dirty
mark behind.

So Inkfinga put his bottle on the floor, and went up to the table
and took the book that Mr. Jack had brought. He turned over all
the pages and looked at all the pictures. Of course he left a smooch
on each. He wiped his fingers on the lace curtains, and then tried to
clean the marks off the book with his handkerchief, but he only
made them worse.

Ethel was so angry that she didn't know what to say. Mr. Jack
knew what to say, but he didn't dare to say it.

"O, Inkfinga!" Ethel said, at last, "how *could* you touch that book
without permission and ruin it?

Are you a Goop?"

(18)

INKFINGA

INKFINGA, a Cherubic Child,
Was never Rough, or Rude, or Wild.
Forbidden Sweets he would not Touch,
Though he might Want them Very Much!
But Oh, Imagination Fails
When I Describe his Finger Nails!

(This Goop is called INKFINGA because his fingers are as
black as ink)

JARDAD was never happy unless he was making a loud noise. He loved to rattle a stick along the balusters, the way Erlydyn did, in the mornings, and everywhere he went he stamped his feet and slammed the doors and yelled and pounded and banged things about.

He has just found an old tin cracker box, and he is making believe it is a drum, pounding away at it with his hammer till Poutine is frightened and has dropped her basket. Quarling has lain down under the sofa, with his sword, behaving unusually well, for him.

Of course, Jardad did n't know that his mother had a sick headache, or he would n't have made so much noise. He ought to have known, for he could see his mother's smelling salts and medicine on the little table.

After he had pounded a hole through the cracker tin, he kicked it downstairs, then he came back and slammed the door, and played with the curtain shade till it flew up with a bang. He made so much noise that he did n't hear his mother when she said,
"Oh, please be a *little* quieter! Why must you make such a racket?

Are you a Goop?"

(20)

JARDAD

Jardad was of those Chosen Few
Who always are both Kind and True;
He did not Interrupt or Tease,
He knew the Proper Way to Sneeze;
He knew the Proper Way, as Well,
To Pound and Rattle, Slam and Yell!

(This Goop is called Jardad because he makes such a
racket as to jar his dad and give his
mother a headache)

THIS lady is Miss Stilcum of Washington; she has a cold, and is eating a cough drop. The Goop with her is Krysoe, who is crying because she will not read to him from his little book. But Miss Stilcum is too busy telling Uncle Harry all about her trip to Europe to listen to this little Goop.

It would n't make much difference if she did, though, for if he is n't crying about one thing, he is crying about another. At school he cried because he could n't feed the goldfish, and he cried at recess because Nevershair would n't give him any of his candy. Then he cried because Miss Stilcum would n't let him take the blacking bottle and paint the beautiful bust that you see on the table.

You see, Uncle Harry had just got Destroya and Rodirtygus to playing cat's cradle, and he thought he could listen in comfort to Miss Stilcum, but Krysoe wanted to play cat's cradle himself, and cried because the other two would n't let him. He doubled up his fists and hopped up and down, like Bawlfred.

Then Uncle Harry got up and said, "what would you think if I made up a face like yours, and cried like a baby? Watch me!"

Uncle Harry looked so funny doing what Krysoe did that they all began to laugh. Miss Stilcum said, "now surely you know what you look like when you cry so.

Are you a Goop?"

(22)

KRYSOE

The little KRYSOE, as a Rule,
Was hardly ever Late to School;
He was as Truthful as could Be,
And Kind to all his Friends was He;
But if he couldn't Have his Way,
He used to Cry almost all Day!

(This Goop is called KRYSOE because he will cry so
if he doesn't get what he wants)

THIS is Jardad's birthday party. Bawlfred is crying under the table because Jardad stepped on his finger. Takim has the mumps, so he is n't here, but Tuchim and the others are playing jackstraws, and it is Ugpert's first turn. She was just ready to draw out a straw very carefully without joggling the other pieces, when Lemeetri crowded in and wanted to do it first. He is saying, "let *me* try! Let *me* try!"

Jardad was too polite to say anything, but Ugpert spoke to Lemeetri very sharply. Miss Curleykew took Lemeetri away from the table and made him sit down on the other side of the room, and wait till his turn came.

Cousin Billy said, "Lemeetri, you are too palestric!" and the minister (who had come in for ice-cream) murmured, "quite so, quite so!"

It was too bad of Lemeetri to act so, for Mr. Jack had only just given him his windmill. Wonty was blowing it to make it go round and round, when Lemeetri ran up and cried, "let *me* try!"

Miss Curleykew went up to Lemeetri after a while and said, "now, are you going to act nicely, or

Are you a Goop?"

LEMEETRI

LEMEETRI was his Mother's Pride—
He could be Lovely, when he Tried;
He Washed his Face, and Combed his Hair
And Put his Things Away with Care;
At Play, his Manners were the Worst—
He always Wished to Do it First!

(This Goop is called LEMEETRI because when he play
a game he always says, "*let* ME *try first!*")

PROFESSOR INCHWORM has been calling on Mark's mother, and has just opened the book he brought last week. It is a book full of colored pictures of insects — he wrote it himself. He has just found a page where, yesterday, a little Goop drew a large man on the clean, white paper. Who do you think did it? Mudfort, of course. Then he forgot all about it until to-day.

Mark Mudfort's mother did n't know what to do, for she had just punished him for marking on the walls, which must be painted over because of his scrawling pictures and letters.

After he was sent out, Mark Mudfort found Yuwanda, who had wandered away from her home as usual. They played out in the yard for a while, and then Mark said, "let's play soldiers in the hall." Yuwanda carefully wiped her feet on the mat, but Mark Mudfort tramped up and down in his muddy boots until the hall was tracked with foot-prints.

Then the professor came out and said, "I have known many queer animals, but you are the queerest I ever saw!

Are you a Goop?"

(26)

MARK MUDFORT

Think of MARK MUDFORT, when you 're Bad!
Think what a Happy Way he Had
Of saying "*Thank you!*"—"*If you Please!*"—
But though so Nice in Things like These,
He Marked on Books and on the Walls—
His Muddy Footprints Marked the Halls!

(This Goop is called MARK MUDFORT because he marks
on things and never wipes the mud off his feet)

NEVERSHAIR was very fond of bananas. So was Verivaine. So were Tuchim and Takim. While these four were playing in the front yard, Nevershair's mother called him in and gave him a large yellow banana. "What have you?" asked Verivaine, when he came out. Nevershair laughed and said, "I've got something I won't tell; nine little niggers in a peanut shell."

"It's a banana," said Tuchim and Takim. Then Nevershair ran off and hid the banana behind his back.

"Give me a bite?" cried Verivaine. "Give me a bite?" cried Tuchim. "Give me a bite?" cried Takim.

"No," said Nevershair. "I am going to eat this banana all myself, and you shan't have any. When I have eaten this banana I am going to get another banana and eat *that* myself, and you shan't have any!"

Nevershair did not see Ethel and Mr. Jack, who came by just then. (Ethel's eyes look as if she had been crying, but she has just promised to marry Mr. Jack and is really very happy.)

"Why, Nevershair," said Ethel, "how can you be so selfish?

Are you a Goop?"

(28)

NEVERSHAIR

To see wee NEVERSHAIR at Work
You'd know he'd never Try to Shirk;
The most Unpleasant Things he'd Do,
If but his Mother Asked him To.
But still, he would n't Lend his Toys
Or Share his Sweets with Other Boys!

(This Goop is called NEVERSHAIR because he will
never share his things with his playmates)

VERISLOW and Olwanoy were having a fine time playing railroad train with the chairs when Obaynotte came in and found them.

"You naughty Goops," he is saying, "don't you know it is wrong to treat the furniture that way? You will scratch the varnish and break the legs." But Verislow and Olwanoy kept on playing. "Get off the track, or you will be run over," Verislow is saying, for he is the engineer.

Obaynotte went out into the back-yard and began to play golf all alone, thinking how naughty these Goops were. When the Goops' mother came in, she found that her best hall chair was broken. So to punish Verislow and Olwanoy she made them sit on the sofa, their hands behind their backs, for half an hour.

Then she raised the window and called for Obaynotte to come in. He kept on playing and pretended not to hear her. When she called again he went further away, so that he could not hear her. Then she said, "Obaynotte, you are as bad as the others!

Are you a Goop?"

OBAYNOTTE

I Fancy that OBAYNOTTE Knew
As much as I, or even You;
He was Too Careful, I am Sure,
To Scratch or Break the Furniture;
He never Squirmed, he never Squalled—
He never Came when he was Called!

(This Goop is called OBAYNOTTE because he does not
obey promptly)

PIEJAM is down
in the cellar, and he
has brought down a
pie and a jar of mar-
malade and two jars
of jam from the
pantry with him.
Katy the Cook has
missed the pies and
sweets, and has come
down into the cel-
lar with Intrupta
and found him.

She is saying, "Oh
Lawks! If it don't
be Piejam, and I sure
thought it was rats! How ever did you get down here, you little Goop?"

Rodirtygus and Haychu were playing in the cellar, but now they
are in the coal-bin and are watching to hear what Katy the Cook
will say. Rodirtygus's face and hands are all black with coal-dust.
Haychu is going to sell all the old bottles for a cent apiece to the
"rags-bottles-sacks" man, when he comes by.

In the afternoon Nibolene came over to see Piejam,
and as they were both extraordinary eaters, you can
easily guess what happened. Piejam had put his
"swagger stick" under his chair and had begun on
a large juicy jar of jam, and Nibolene was eating her
fourth doughnut, when Piejam's mother came in.

"Piejam," she said, "to-day, to my certain knowl-
edge, you have eaten, between meals, at least two tons
of Goop-food.

*Are you a
Goop?"*

(32)

PIEJAM

Just Fancy PIEJAM for a Name!
Yet he was Honest, just the Same;
For PIEJAM never, never Lied,
And PIEJAM never, never Cried—
And Yet he was a Greedy Pig—
His Appetite was Much Too Big!

(This Goop is called PIEJAM because he eats so much
pie and jam and candy)

When Quarling went out to play, he found Hatesope and Rudella down the road. First they shot at the fence with Rudella's bow and arrows, and she did the best. Then they played "three old cats" with Hatesope's bat and ball, and Hatesope did the best. Then they ran races, and Quarling did the best.

Then Quarling said, " let's play soldiers, and I will be the captain, for I have a sword." So he marched Rudella and Hatesope up and down the sidewalk.

Quarling said to Hatesope, "you don't keep in step, and you don't carry your gun right." Hatesope said, "you are out of step yourself, and you don't carry your sword right."

Then Quarling got angry and hit Hatesope with his sword, and frightened Rudella so she screamed. The policeman came across the street and said to Quarling, "you are quarrelling again, I see; I'll have to attend to you!"

Quarling was very much frightened, but then he saw his mother coming, and he was very much ashamed of having behaved so badly. When she came up, she said to him, "Quarling, you are in-cor-rig-i-ble!

Are you a Goop?"

QUARLING

You'd Love to See quaint QUARLING Go
On Errands, for he Liked to, so;
All Kinds of Work he'd Bravely Try,
For he was Quick and he was Spry.
He was so Spry, I Grieve to Say,
He often Quarrelled at his Play.

(This Goop is called QUARLING because he is always
quarrelling)

WHEN Mr. Jack's mother came to call on Ethel, she said, "now I want to see the children, for I've heard so much about them."

So Ethel called Lazileva and Mudfort and Rodirtygus down from the nursery.

Lazileva was spick and span and clean, for she washed her face and hands before she came down. She made a lovely little curtsey, and Mrs. Jack said, "what a deliciously dainty child; she looks as if she had just come home from the milliner's in a bandbox!"

Mudfort was spick and span and clean (all except his boots), for he had washed his face and hands before he came down. He made a low bow, and Mrs. Jack said, "what a delightfully decent child; he looks as if he were made in a toy shop, and had just been varnished!" (She didn't notice his boots.)

But Rodirtygus had been playing with some clay, and he was all over mud, hands and face and clothes and everything. He had forgotten to wash himself before he came down. He took off his hat and smiled pleasantly, and Mrs. Jack said, "what a dismally dirty child; he looks as if he had been thrown into the ash barrel and had been taken out by mistake. Tell me,

Are you a Goop?"

RODIRTYGUS

Rᴏᴅɪʀᴛʏɢᴜs was Meek and Mild,
He Softly Spoke, he Sweetly Smiled;
He never Called his Playmates Names,
He was Polite when Playing Games;
But he was often in Disgrace
Because he Had a Dirty Face!

(This Goop is called Rᴏᴅɪʀᴛʏɢᴜs because he is always
so dirty)

Sulkie never really disobeys his parents, but when he is asked to do anything he does n't want to do, he sulks so badly that it is almost as bad as if he refused outright, the way Wonty does. He scowls and frowns and whines and whimpers and scuffs his feet and hangs back.

This picture shows the yard of the house where Sulkie lives. The Hotel Goop, that Cousin Billy made, is over behind the trees, near where Nibolene is playing tether-ball. Urapyg is running across the lawn shouting that the hotel is on fire, and he wants to use the express-wagon for a fire-engine. Of course the hotel is not really on fire. He is only playing that it is.

Quirita has been pulling Sulkie up and down the board walk in the wagon, for she would rather be the horse than the driver. Sulkie has been having so much fun that when Cousin Billy came out on the steps and told him it was time for him to come in and go to bed, he began to sulk, as usual (just like Whymusty and Dowanto).

" I don't see why I have to come in now," he whined, but he got down very slowly with a very unpleasant expression on his face, hanging back as long as he dared.

" You know you have had a sore throat," Cousin Billy said, " and it is getting cold and damp, so you ought to be in the house. Why can't you obey willingly and cheer-fully, instead of sulking so ?

Are you a Goop? "

SULKIE

What SULKIE Borrowed, he Returned,
And Many were the Thanks he Earned
By Leaving Others' Things Alone,
Remembering they were Not his Own;
Yet he was Sulky, so They Say,
When not Allowed to Have his Way!

(This Goop is called SULKIE because if he can't do what
he wishes to, or has to do what he *does n't*
wish, he is sulky)

TUCHIM has just been up in his father's room, and has carried away his watch and his best razor to play with, and Takim has just been up in his mother's room, and has taken away her opera-glasses; and when they have finished playing with them, they will probably leave them in the bath-tub. Yellkum and Stinjessie are looking on, knowing that the twins are going to get into trouble.

The picture below shows another of their scrapes. Father was reading quietly in the library. Tuchim got up on a rocking-chair and reached for the candy, while Takim stepped up on the foot of the table and got it first. Then Tuchim's chair rocked and threw him over, and as he fell he knocked over the lamp, and spilled a glass of water, a can of liquid glue, and a bottle of ink. They all came down together on the floor. Father was just too late to catch them, and was so provoked at the mischief the twins had made that he said, "I never saw so ill-bred a child as you, Tuchim, unless it is you, Takim:

Are you a Goop!"

TUCHIM & TAKIM

TUCHIM and TAKIM were a Pair
Who Acted Nicely Everywhere;
They Studied hard, as Good as Gold,
They always Did as they were Told;
But I have Caught Them Unawares
Meddling with Things that were not Theirs!

(These Goops are called TUCHIM and TAKIM because
they touch and take things that are not theirs)

THIS shows the Hotel Goop that Cousin Billy built out of a packing-case. It is fitted up like a little house inside, with a carpet on the floor, and pictures on the walls, and a table and shelves and two chairs. Zelphina is sweeping and dusting it out, as she expects Xcitabelle to call on her this morning.

Urapyg and Nevershair wanted to play "fire," so they got Cousin Billy to set up the ladder against a clothes-pole. Then Cousin Billy sat down on the grass and waited for Miss Curleykew.

Just as she came out with Xcitabelle, Nevershair ran up to the top of the ladder, and Urapyg was angry, because he had wanted to go up first. He said, "I am the chief, for I have a fireman's helmet, and I ought to go first. You're a pig to go first,

and I won't play any more!"

Miss Curleykew was surprised to hear him use such horrid words, and she said, "Urapyg, you'll have to wash your mouth out with soap, if you use such bad words.

Are you a Goop?"

(42)

URAPYG

Young URAPYG took Good Advice,
And always Kept his Clothing Nice;
He never Smooched his Frock with Coal,
His Picture Books were Clean and Whole;
He Washed his Hands Ten Times a Day —
But OH! What Horrid Things he'd Say!

(This Goop is called URAPYG because he says bad words
and calls names; once he said to his sister,
"you're a pig!")

MOTHER was expecting the minister to dinner, and she wanted to cook something very good to eat, as the minister was very fond of food. So she made some sweet soup, and mealy meat-balls, and various vegetables, and prime pudding, and pleasant pie for dinner. But what the minister liked best was home-made bread, for where he lived they got all their bread at a bakery.

So she sent Verislow out for a yeast cake early in the afternoon, and told him to come back quickly. But Verislow was so much interested in looking at the pictures on the circus posters that he was a long time getting to the grocery-store, and on his way back he found Piejam and Fijetta playing with a new purple toy balloon.

He stayed with them for a whole hour, until Fijetta lost her balloon, and it sailed away in the air. Verislow forgot all about the yeast cake, until his mother came out to the kitchen door, in great anxiety.

"O Verislow," she cried, "you are so late I won't have time to make any home-made bread for the minister!

Are you a Goop?"

(44)

VERISLOW

No Doubt that VERISLOW was Such
As Casual Callers Flatter Much;
His Maiden Aunts would Say, with Glee,
"*How Good, How Sweet, how Dear is He!*"
And yet, he Drove his Mother Crazy —
He *was* so Slow, he *was* so Lazy!

(This Goop is called VERISLOW because he is so very
slow in doing what he is told to do)

THIS fat man is Mr. Jack's father, and Ethel loves to have him call, because he is always so good-natured and jolly. Nothing ever disturbs him. When Teeza teased to be allowed to sit up to the table and write a letter, old Mr. Jack gave her a pencil out of his own pocket to use. When Dowanto lost his kite, old Mr. Jack laid down his book and looked all over the house till he found the kite for him.

But there is one thing that old Mr. Jack doesn't like, and that is disobedience. He hates to hear children whine, and he hates to see them sulk, and Whymusty does both.

First, Ethel told Whymusty that he must go upstairs and have his face washed, and Whymusty began to scowl, and said, "why must I?" Then old Mr. Jack looked up over his glasses and shook his head.

Next, Ethel told Whymusty that he was making so much noise playing soldier and yelling "bang!!!" when he shot off his gun that he must go out in the hall and play, for he was disturbing them. Whymusty said, "why must I?" Old Mr. Jack shook his head again.

Then at last Ethel asked Whymusty to go out and bring in the hammock, because it looked like rain, and Whymusty said, "why must I?"

So old Mr. Jack said, "Whymusty, if you dress like a soldier you must act like a soldier, and soldiers always obey orders without a question. But if you're not really a soldier, what are you?

Are you a Goop?"

WHYMUSTY

Don't Think that WHYMUSTY was Ill
Because he Sometimes Kept so Still—
He Knew his Mother did not Care
To Hear him Talking Everywhere.
He did not Hint, he did not Cry,
But he was Always Asking "WHY?"

(This Goop is called WHYMUSTY because when he is
asked to do anything he asks, "WHY *must I?*")

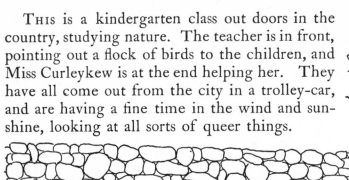

THIS is a kindergarten class out doors in the country, studying nature. The teacher is in front, pointing out a flock of birds to the children, and Miss Curleykew is at the end helping her. They have all come out from the city in a trolley-car, and are having a fine time in the wind and sunshine, looking at all sorts of queer things.

They have all behaved nicely except Xaspery, who has done everything he can to annoy his teacher. He ran away down the road after a butterfly, instead of walking quietly in order beside Sulkie, and he snatched at Messalina's spoon and threw it over the stone wall, and he never listened to what the teacher said, but asked, "what was it?" when she had finished explaining something. He was so exasperating in school to-day that his teacher would not let him take his alpenstock out with him, although you see Mudfort has his spear and Zeemsneaze his drum.

Xaspery has just found a worm, and he is so busy looking at it that he does n't see the flying birds. Then he looked up too late to see the birds and said, "where are they?" His teacher said to him, "why are you always so heedless and inattentive?

Are you a Goop?"

XASPERY

When Xaspery *Tried* to be Polite,
They Called him Gentlemanly, Quite;
His Manners were Correct and Nice,
He Never Asked for Jelly Twice.
Still, when he Tried to Misbehave,
Oh, How much Trouble Xaspery Gave!

(This Goop is called Xaspery because he exasperates his
parents and teachers with his misbehavior
and inattention)

This is Yellkum's mother's reception day. Krysoe was asked to come in and show how well he could read for the visitors, and he came in such a hurry that he forgot to put on one shoe. He read, "Do we go up? We do go up. The hen is on the bed." Then Jotantrum recited "How to Eat Soup," and forgot only half of it. The two Misses Wigglesworth said that both were charming, and Dr. Golosher that his memory was just like Jotantrum's. Young Mr. Snale said they both were " very unique." Then they had tea and began to talk gubble all together. Gubble is the language of tea-parties.

Mother was telling what a time she was having with the housemaid when they heard a great noise out in the hall, and Yellkum burst into the room yelling, " Back Bay Station! This train for Baltimore, Toledo, and Northwest Territory! Passengers for Honolulu, Paris, and Asia Minor please change cars! Twenty minutes for refreshments. Beware of pickpockets! Next stop Thirty-Second Street!" Then he began to pound on the piano with his shovel.

Young Mr. Snale was so frightened that he nearly dropped his cup and saucer. Ethel came into the room just then, and she said: "Why I haven't heard such a noise since I was in the Midway Plaisance, Yellkum, Are you a huckster, or

Are you a Goop?"

YELLKUM

Young YELLKUM was a Merry Boy,
Who Filled his Sister's Heart with Joy—
For he would Always Give her Half
Of all his Goodies, with a Laugh;
Yet I prefer Mild-Mannered Boys
Who do not Make such *Awful* Noise!

(This Goop is called YELLKUM because he yells so loudly)

THE Goops did not like the minister much, because he always said, "and how is my little man to-day?" But when Ethel asked them to come in, they had to go because their mother said they must. She was too tired, herself.

Abednego and Badinskool behaved beautifully, even when the minister pointed his glasses at them and smiled, though they would much rather be out playing than telling how old they were, what they learned in school, and how they liked their teacher. But while the minister was talking to him, Zeemsneaze disgraced himself by wiping his nose on his sleeve. Ethel was shocked. The minister said, "where is your handkerchief, my little man?" Zeemsneaze had left it in the stable, and had n't used it all day! When they went up to Miss Curleykew's room, and told her about it, she said, "why Zeemsneaze, you are as bad as a horse!

Are you a Goop?"

ZEEMSNEAZE

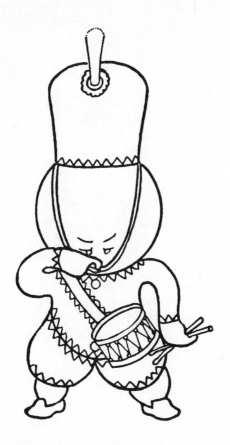

Oh, Laugh at Zeemsneaze if you Will
But he was Brave when he was Ill,
When he was Ill he was so Brave
He Swallowed all his Mother Gave;
And so, you Scarcely will Believe
He Wiped his Nose upon his Sleeve!

(This Goop is called Zeemsneaze because when you see
him sneeze, you *don't* see his handkerchief!)

(53)

ELOSTUM and Erlydyn are allowed to
stay in the room with Ethel and Mr. Jack,
to-day, because they were playing a "quiet" game.
They are talking in signs, and the one who speaks first
has to pay a forfeit.

But when Askalotte came in she began to talk as fast
as she could. This is what she said: "Eth-el, why aren't you talking to Mr. Jack any more? Are you mad with Mr. Jack? Mr. Jack,
why do you look so cross? Are you mad with Ethel? Ethel, where
is your ring? Aren't you going to wear your ring any more? Eth-el,
if Mr. Jack made you mad what would you do? Mr. Jack, who was
that lady you were with yesterday? How old is she, Mr. Jack? Eth-el,
did you see the lady Mr. Jack was with? Mr. Jack, did you take
away Ethel's ring? Is it in your pocket? Aren't you going to give it
back to her any more? Are you going to give it to that lady, Mr.
Jack? Eth-el, are you going to church with Mr. Jack to-morrow?
Are you, Ethel? Mr. Jack, do you think Ethel is pretty? Do you
think she is as pretty as that lady you were with yesterday, Mr. Jack?"

At last Ethel and Mr. Jack both burst out laughing at the silly
questions. Ethel looked at Mr. Jack and said, "I really think Askalotte is a Goop, and I *know* I am one, sometimes.

Are you a Goop?"

ASKALOTTE

Children, Behold Miss ASKALOTTE,
A most Attractive little Tot;
She was not Rude, nor yet Unkind,
I Never Knew her Not to Mind;
Yet she was always Asking Questions,
And Making most Ill-Timed Suggestions.

(This Goop is called ASKALOTTE because she asks such a
lot of needless questions)

HERE are some of the things that Badinskool did to annoy her kindergarten teacher: she played, instead of working, she whispered and talked when she should have been listening to her teacher, she got out of line when she was marching, she pounded on the table, she tipped over backwards in her chair, and she scuffed her feet on the floor.

When they all pulled up their chairs into a circle and began to sing "Thumbkin says, 'I'll dance,'" Badinskool saw a bird on a tree. "I want to be a bird!" she said, and began to fly round the room like a bird, waving her arms like wings.

Then the teacher took her from the circle and made her sit in her chair by herself, till Badinskool said she would behave better.

Afterward, when all the children were making mice out of clay, Badinskool rolled up little balls of clay and threw them at Hatesope and Fibius, then she pinched Jotantrum's little clay mouse till it was all out of shape. So, because she had been so naughty, the teacher would not give Badinskool any little clay mouse to take home.

Are you a Goop?

BADINSKOOL

Though BADINSKOOL was often Hurt,
She did not Cry—nor was she Pert.
She was as Generous as could Be,
And None was more Refined than She;
So it is odd that, when in School,
She acted Badly, as a Rule!

(This Goop is called BADINSKOOL because she acts so
badly in school)

CAROLESSE is the most heedless and careless Goop that ever lived. As she came downstairs, she saw Fibius going on an errand. She threw up the window and called to him, but forgot to put the window down again. It was raining and blowing, so the pretty crisp lace curtains flew out and got wet, and the rain came in and soaked the rug.

Then she dropped her doll, and left it where it lay, because she heard Abednego coming in. He had been to see the circus. She ran downstairs and did n't notice the flower-pot on the table, and knocked it over upon the floor. She tripped on the mat and fell against a little table and upset that, too. A vase that belonged to Askalotte was broken, and Askalotte, who has heard the noise, is coming downstairs to see what is the matter.

Her mother has been counting the careless things Carolesse has done. "One, two, three, four, five! Mercy's sakes alive!" she said. "And you have broken Jotantrum's fan, too, that makes six; just because you can *never* be careful and take heed what you do! Think what you 're doing and look where you go, then you 'll be spared all your worry and woe! If you are not a Goop you 'll learn that, and practise it.

Are you a Goop?"

(58)

CAROLESSE

If CAROLESSE was Spoiled, a Bit,
I'm Sure I never Heard of It;
She always Did as she was Told,
She did not Whine, she did not Scold;
But she was Careless, Everywhere—
Her Mother found it Hard to Bear!

(This Goop is called CAROLESSE because she is so
careless)

THIS is Destroya cutting out pictures of animals to paste into her circus scrap-book. Her father has given her some newspapers and an old magazine to cut up. She is trying to have a picture of every kind of animal in her book. Badinskool is coming to draw the picture of a lion on her slate.

If Destroya cut out pictures only from the books and papers that were given to her, she would never get into trouble, but ever since she was a baby she has liked to tear pages out of books, and cut up papers with her scissors. Just now she is hunting for a picture of a bear, because she needs one for her circus book.

As Destroya could n't find one, she looked through all the books in her father's library. Then Jardad told her that there was one in a book called "Farthest North" on the table. Destroya took it down and found a be—autiful bear, and cut it out and pasted it into her own book. Then she cut out a fox and a seal and an albatross and some other strange animals.

In the lower picture, you see Father has just found his book. Mother gave it to him for Christmas, and now it is ruined. He is saying, "Destroya, I shall have to take away your scissors and your circus book for a week! I *thought* you were a little lady.

Are you a Goop?"

DESTROYA

You'd never Think, to See DESTROYA,
That Anything could much Annoy her;
She'd Lend her Toys, she'd Help her Brother,
She'd Run on Errands for her Mother;
But Books and Papers, Every Day,
She'd Tear, in quite an Awful Way!

(This Goop is called DESTROYA because she destroys
so many things)

ERLYDYN always wakes up early in the morning and comes into her Mother's room and wakes her up. No matter how tired or sleepy poor Mother is, there is no more sleep for her after that. This morning Erlydyn was worse than usual. She got up at five o'clock and came in and jumped on Mother's bed. Then she crawled into the bed and teased her Mother for a story. Then she wanted to play that she was a

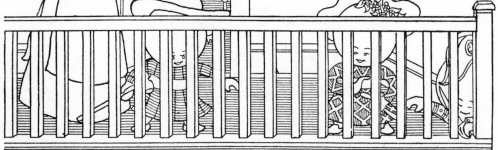

kitten, and that her Mother was the mother cat. Then she wanted to be a little dog, and she crawled way down inside the bed-clothes and barked. Then she got out of bed and brought her woolly sheep and made it squeak "baa—baaa!" Then she wanted to play horse with Mother, and use Mother's braided hair for the reins.

Finally, Erlydyn got up and dressed herself; then, when she found her croquet mallet, she thought she would make believe that the balusters were a piano and play on them with the mallet.

She is making a terrific noise, while Messalina and Nevershair, who have been up for some time, are playing quietly; for they know that Ethel was out late at a dance last night, and wants to sleep as long as she can. Mary is taking some breakfast to Uncle Harry's room, for he has to catch the 6.15 train.

Father has just come to the door in his pajamas, and he is saying, "Erlydyn, please let me sleep a *little* longer. I dreamed that there was an awful thunder storm; but it was only you!

Are you a Goop?"

(62)

ERLYDYN

See ERLYDYN, a Cunning Miss,
Whom Everybody Longed to Kiss.
She was so Sweet, she was so Clever,
She Needed Scolding Scarcely Ever.
Yet she would Rise at Six o'Clock
And Wake her Parents with a Shock!

(This Goop is called ERLYDYN because she gets up early
and makes such a din that no one can sleep)

FIJETTA and Olwaynoy and Quarling are going to have their photographs taken by Cousin Billy. Mother has had a hard time with Quarling who has been quarrelling with Olwaynoy, and so now to punish him Mother has made him sit quietly in a chair until all three are ready. If he gets out of the chair or speaks once he will not have his photograph taken. Olwaynoy has behaved as badly, and now she is hiding Fijetta's stockings.

But Mother is having almost as bad a time with Fijetta, who simply will *not* keep still while she is being dressed. First, she kept reaching for her beads which were on the bureau, and then she threw them on the floor, and began trying to get her hat. While Mother was putting her shirt on she kept clapping her hands, and while Mother was trying to button it up, she jumped up and down. Nellie the nursemaid has just washed and ironed Fijetta's frock and is ready to put it on for her. Mother is almost out of patience with this little Goop, because she fidgets when she is being washed and combed and dressed every morning so that it always takes a long time to dress her.

When Cousin Billy came in to find out what was delaying them, he said, "Oh, I didn't know I was going to make a Goop photograph! What's the matter, Fijetta,

Are you a Goop?"

(64)

FIJETTA

Fijetta never Disobeyed,
She never Quarrelled when she Played;
She never Scowled, or Shook her Head,
When it was Time to Go to Bed.
But *How* she Fidgetted, while Dressing!
Her Mother found it *Most* Distressing.

(This Goop is called Fijetta because she fidgets so
while her mother is dressing her)

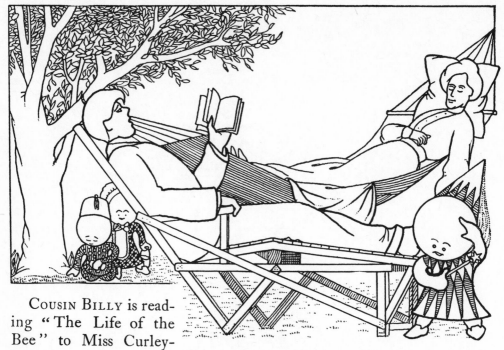

Cousin Billy is reading "The Life of the Bee" to Miss Curleykew, in a shady corner of the orchard. He is sitting in a queer chair that he made himself. Miss Curleykew is almost asleep.

Askalotte, Poutine and Inkfinga have been out picking berries, and have just come home. Poutine has a quart of blueberries in her pail. Inkfinga is pouring out the milk that was left in his bottle into the dirt, and he will soon go into the house with muddy hands.

Gablia is telling Cousin Billy all about her walk, talking as fast as she can, although he does n't want to listen to it now, as he is interested in his book. Gablia is a Goop, however, and keeps right on talking so that he can't read. She is saying:

"We had an *awful* good time and we picked a quart of blueberries and we ate them half up and we drank the milk and I saw two cows and I was n't afraid *at all*, but Poutine was and Inkfinga threw a stick at them and they ran away and then we went in wading in the brook and Carolesse came along and dropped her doll —"

"Never mind, now," Cousin Billy is saying, "I want to read!"

"But we had to fish the doll out of the brook," Gablia went on.

"It's very interesting," Cousin Billy said, "but if you'll talk it into my phonograph I'll listen to it later. I'm busy, now. Are you going to run away and leave us alone, or

Are you a Goop?"

GABLIA

I'm Sure you all Know GABLIA Well —
Her Virtues, then, I Need not Tell.
In Praise of her, it Might be Said
She Was Exceedingly Well-Bred;
Well Bred she was, yet Talked Too Much.
I Think you May have Heard of Such!

(This Goop is called GABLIA because she talks and
gabbles all the time when no one wants to
listen to her)

THIS is a golf tournament, and Ethel is driving from the third hole. Miss Stilcum of Washington has just driven off, and Uncle Harry is over the other side of the hill, telling Ethel which way to drive. Mr. Jack is just coming up, but you can't see him yet.

They all went out to the links in an electric car together, taking Haychu and Obaynotte with them. These two little Goops quarrelled all the way out. Haychu wanted the end seat, and when Ethel told her she must sit inside, she said to Obaynotte, "you are mean not to give me the end seat when we got in! You are a nelephant, and I hate you!"

They found Hatesope out at the links, and as he wanted to be Ethel's caddy, she is letting him carry her clubs.

Obaynotte is teaching Haychu to play golf, but she won't listen; she wants to try herself, before she knows how. She is calling Obaynotte all sorts of horrid names because he won't let her take his clubs.

Then, at last, when she tried to use the clubs Obaynotte laughed at her, and she lost her temper. "You are an old niblick, that's what you are, and I hate you!" she said. When Obaynotte told her he would show her how, she said, "go away! I hate you!"

When Cousin Billy came round to where they were, he heard Haychu saying to Obaynotte, "I'll slap your face for you, you horrid thing, I hate you!" He felt very badly to think that she would talk so, and he said, "if you knew how ugly you looked when you spoke so angrily, you would never do it again. You look as ugly as a Goop.

Are you a Goop?"

HAYCHU

When Happy, HAYCHU was so Sweet
Some Thought her Good enough to Eat!
To Witness HAYCHU's Happy Smile
Was Singularly Worth one's While!
Yet Oft, when Angry, HAYCHU said
Some Things Considered *Not* Well Bred!

(This Goop is called HAYCHU because when she's cross
she says horrid things, like: " *I hate you!* ")

As it is nearly time for Ethel and Mr. Jack to be married, they are making out a list of the wedding invitations. Krysoe is listening and saying nothing. Teeza is making a ball out of string. But Intrupta is giving a great deal of trouble by asking needless questions and interrupting Ethel and Mr. Jack while they are talking. This is the way she annoys them:

ETHEL: Now there's Professor Inchworm; I wonder if we ought—

INTRUPTA: Eth-el, where is my jump-rope?

ETHEL: There it is on the floor right in front of you. I suppose we really ought to invite him.

MR. JACK: I don't know, if we only did n't have so many relatives—

INTRUPTA: Can I go to school to-morrow without my jacket on?

ETHEL: *Do* run away and play, please. Of course, if we have Cousin Billy at the ceremony, we *must* have Miss Curleykew. Do you know—

INTRUPTA: Gablia's going to school without a jacket. Can't I?

MR. JACK: Yes, I have been wondering if it were n't time for it to be announced. If Harry would only come to the point—

INTRUPTA: Eth-el! do you know where Fibius is?

ETHEL: It *would* be a good chance for a double wedding, would n't it? Now what are we going to do with Grandfather? Somebody will have—

INTRUPTA: Eth-el! can I have a party to-morrow?

ETHEL: — to take him to the church. No, dear, wait until your birthday. Why *won't* you let us talk!

Are you a Goop?

(70)

INTRUPTA

INTRUPTA's Infant History
Was Full of Deepest Mystery;
For, Knowing, as she Did, the Way
To be so Good, at Work or Play,
WHY did she often Interrupt
Her Seniors, in a Style Abrupt?

(This Goop is called INTRUPTA because she interrupts
persons when they are talking)

JOTANTRUM is having one of her tantrums — right out on the street, too! It happened this way. Her mother came out and got into the carriage to go calling. Jotantrum wanted to go with her. "No," said Mother, "not to-day." Then Jotantrum stamped her foot on the ground so hard that she fell over and lay on her back kicking and screaming with all her might. "I want to go! I want to go!" she cried.

Just then Verislow and Haychu came by and said, "come along with us! We are going to sail boats in the pond."

"I won't go! I want to go to ride with my mother," the little Goop screamed. Verislow and Haychu were so horrified to see her act this way that they walked off and left her.

This made Jotantrum angrier still. Then a little dog came up and began to bark at her. Jotantrum got up then and hit the dog with her fan, and the little dog snapped at her so that she was frightened and ran in the house.

When Nelly the nurse saw Jotantrum's dress all covered with dust she said, "now you must be washed, and put on a clean frock." Then the little Goop had another tantrum. She screamed and kicked so hard that you could hear her for nearly a block away.

Charles the coachman is saying to Frank the footman, "Frank, this off horse has only three legs! He must be a Goop horse!

Are you a Goop?"

JOTANTRUM

JOTANTRUM Normally was Nice.
They did not Have to Call her Twice,
For she would Cheerfully Obey
In Quite a Willing Sort of Way.
She *Usually* Did So, I Mean—
Sometimes, she Made an Awful Scene!

(This Goop is called JOTANTRUM because when she
is disappointed she screams and flies into a tantrum)

KORLAWAY has been put to bed, and Cousin Billy and Father and Mother and Miss Curley-kew are playing a quiet game of whist. They were all settled, and Mother had just found ten trumps in her hand, when they heard the first goop-call.

"Ma-ma! I want a drink of water!"

So Mother had to leave the game and go upstairs. She had just come down and had begun playing again, when Korlaway called,

"Ma-ma! Come up and pull the clothes over me!" After that had been done, she called out, "Ma-ma! Come and tell me a story!" The next time it was "Ma-ma! When are you coming to bed?"

Father was just telling how well he played the last hand, when Korlaway was heard again:

"Ma-ma! Come kiss me!"

And Mother is saying, "no, I don't want to kiss Goops to-night!

Are you a Goop?"

KORLAWAY

Oh, Have you Seen Miss KORLAWAY,
So Blithe, so Happy, and so Gay?
How Cheerfully she Helped her Ma,
Or Brought his Slippers for her Pa!
But when in Bed, or at her Play,
She'd Call them Both from Far Away!

(This Goop is called KORLAWAY because she calls her
parents from their work or reading when
it is not necessary)

LAZILEVA was the kind of Goop who would leave her tricycle out on the sidewalk when she came in, because she was in too much of a hurry to put it away in the cellar; and by the time she went to look for it, it would be gone.

This picture shows how Lazileva had all the furniture of her doll's house broken. After luncheon she decided to clean house. So she took all the chairs and tables out of the bed-room and the dining-room and the parlor of her house, and put them on the floor. Then she got a little whisk-broom from behind the bath-room door, and began to sweep the carpets of her little house. While she was washing the windows, Cawlomar came in and asked her to go out and play squat-tag with him and Gablia. So she went out and left her things all lying about on the floor.

While they were playing they saw the Minister coming to call. Mother called out the window for them to ask him into the sitting-room. You see what happened! He did not see Lazileva's furniture on the floor, and he is walking right over them with his heavy boots! When Mother came down she found Lazileva crying, and she said to her, "what kind of a child are you, to leave your things all scattered about so?

Are you a Goop?"

LAZILEVA

Though LAZILEVA's Frocks were Neat,
Her Manners Good, her Words Discreet,
Although she did not Talk Too Much,
And did not Meddle, Taste, or Touch,
Yet Scarce a Child could e'er be Found
Who Left so Many Things Around!

(This Goop is called LAZILEVA because she is so lazy
that she leaves her things about instead of
putting them where they belong)

THESE Goops were invited to a party at Xcitabelle's house one afternoon, and Messalina was so much in a hurry to go that she asked to be dressed first. So she *was* dressed first, and her mother put some fresh flowers in her hat. The day before, Messalina had been out in the rain and the color had washed out of the flowers and stained her face so red and green that everybody called her a Goop.

When Messalina was dressed, she took the old flowers and went out in the garden to plant them. She dug a hole in the dirt with her wooden spoon and stuck the flowers into it, and made such a mess that soon her face and her hands and her frock were very dirty.

So, when Ethel and Mr. Jack came out with Korlaway and Yellkum to go to the party, they found Messalina had to be washed and dressed all over again! Mr. Jack went on with Korlaway and Yellkum, while Ethel took Messalina back into the house.

Messalina had soiled her white slippers so badly that she had to wear her old black ones to the party; and she got there too late to get any ice-cream. And she cried.

"It's your own fault," Ethel said to her, "for if you hadn't made such a mess after you were dressed, you would have been on time.

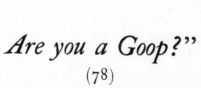

Are you a Goop?"

(78)

MESSALINA

Miss MESSALINA, as you See,
Was Just as Pretty as Could Be!
She never, never, never Cried,
She *couldn't* Do it if she Tried!
But, if she Tried, she *Could* Make Messes
That Spoiled her Lovely Clean Fresh Dresses!

(This Goop is called MESSALINA because she makes
messes that spoil her clothes)

Cousin Billy called Nibolene an "enthusiastic two-handed eater." She was always eating something, usually a doughnut. She ate so much between meals that she seldom had any appetite at the table.

In the picture below the dressmaker is making Ethel's clothes for the wedding. She has been telling fairy stories to Zeemsneaze and Xcitabelle. Minnie the maid is bringing her a pot of tea.

Nibolene has just come in and has told about a lovely cake with white frosting that she found in the pantry. "Did you nibble any of it?" the dressmaker asked. Nibolene had to confess that she did.

"I thought so," said the dressmaker, "and you have bitten your own nose off, that's what you have done! To-morrow is your birthday and your mother was going to give you a surprise party. The cake was for a birthday cake, and it was going to have five candles on it, for you will be five years old to-morrow. But now, of course, you will have no party because you have no cake. It seems to me you are fond of Goop food.

"You should never eat anything between meals without asking your mother's consent. I knew a little girl once who was so greedy that she ate a whole cake. It was an April Fool cake, filled with sawdust; but she was so greedy she never noticed it. She was a Goop.

Are you a Goop?"

NIBOLENE

Ah, Nibolene, Sweet Nibolene,
Was Neat and Spick and Span and Clean!
She Told the Truth, Indeed she Did,
And Always Did as she was Bid;
So, I am Rather Sorry that
She Ate so Much she soon grew Fat!

(This Goop is called Nibolene because she is always
nibbling and eating between meals)

THIS is May-day, and these children are twining a
May-pole, dancing round and round and in and out, till all the ribbons
are twisted on the pole. Cousin Billy got up the party; he chose the
children and taught them how to do it.

Now, Olwaynoy wanted to be one of them very much, but Cousin
Billy would n't have her because she teased and annoyed the others so
much. She got very angry because she could n't dance, and while
they were twining the pole with the ribbons, she ran away from her
mother, and did her best to spoil the dance.

She pinched them as they went by, and she tripped them up; she
pushed them and she snatched at what they were carrying. She took
their hats and threw them over the fence. Finally, she threw a piece
of dirt at Yuwanda.

Then Cousin Billy stopped the dance and had Olwaynoy taken
home and sent to bed, and so she missed the Punch-and-Judy show,
and the lemonade and ice-cream and cake. Olwaynoy is about the
worst of all the Goops. She always does a thing *once* more, after you
tell her to stop! She certainly is a Goop!

Are you a Goop?

OLWAYNOY

What do you Think of OLWAYNOY?
She was as Brave as any Boy!
If she Fell down, she Scorned to Cry.
She never Told a single Lie!
Yet she has Teased her Little Brothers
Her Pussy-Cat, and Many Others!

(This Goop is called OLWANOY because she is always
annoying her playmates and pets)

ETHEL and Mr. Jack, in the row boat, and Cousin Billy and Miss Curleykew in the canoe, are going up the river to get Uncle Harry and Miss Stilcum, who are at the club house. When they come back, they are all going to have a picnic under the trees beside the river.

Verislow is sailing his boat with Fijetta. They have both taken off their shoes and stockings and put them on a rock. Verislow is so afraid that his boat will be run down that he is shouting to Mr. Jack to look out for it. Fijetta is shouting, too.

Poutine came up the river with Ethel and Mr. Jack in the row boat, and when they got here, Ethel made Poutine get out and wait on the bank for them, for there would not be room for her in the boat, when Uncle Harry and Miss Stilcum got in. Poutine is very cross at being left behind. She got out slowly and sulkily, and made an awful face. She said, "I should think you *might* take me up the river. It's *mean!*"

Ethel and Mr. Jack are laughing at Poutine, for she is pouting and scowling, as she always does when she can't have her own way.

"I *want* to go!" Poutine said. "I don't want to stay here *at all!*"

Ethel only smiled at her and said, "remember the picnic we are going to have when we come back! Goops will not be allowed at our picnic;

Are you a Goop?"

(84)

POUTINE

Behold Poutine, the Brightest Lass
Of all her Kindergarten Class!
She was Polite and Truthful, Too,
And Did what she was Told to Do,
Yet Often Did it with a Face
That Robbed Poutine of Half her Grace!

(This Goop is called Poutine because she pouts and
scowls when she can't have her own way)

THE Goop Family are having supper, and Matthew, the Minister's son, has come in with Ethel to see them. Lazileva is late, of course. She put off washing her face and hands till the supper-bell rang. Inkfinga came in a hurry, but he did n't remember to wash at all! Mary the maid is bringing in a potato pie.

Matthew the Minister's son is staring at Quirita, because he never saw anybody eat so queerly in his life. She is eating a whole cream-cake at one bite, and you will soon see the cream all over her face where it has squirted out. I hate to think of it. Nelly the nurse has already had to take away Quirita's mug, for she put her fingers in it, and when it was emptied, she threw her head back and tried to balance the mug on her face.

Quirita gobbled and gugged. She made shocking noises, and *all* the time she was not eating she played with her knife or fork or spoon or the salt or her napkin ring, instead of keeping her hands in her lap the way Ethel does. She blew and bubbled into the water when she drank out of her glass, she squeaked her knife on her plate, and she reached out and took the strawberries from the dish with her fingers!

Matthew is saying, "I suppose, Miss Ethel, Quirita should be considered as essentially mediæval in her manners." What he means is, that Quirita is a Goop.

Are you a Goop?

QUIRITA

She has a Funny Name——Quirita!
Yet Never Little Girl was Sweeter.
So Seldom was she Found to Blame
You'll Wonder How she Got her Name——
But if you Dined with her, you'd Know;
Her Table Manners, they were Low!

(This Goop is called Quirita because she is such a
queer eater, and has no manners at table)

THIS very good-looking young man is Mr. Jimmie Bimm, who is to be the best man when Mr. Jack is married to Ethel. Mr. Jack is introducing him to Ethel's mother.

Jimmie Bimm would enjoy his call better if it was n't for Rudella. She has been acting so rudely that he scarcely knows what to say. Rudella pranced across right in front of him while he was saying to Ethel's mother, "I thought you were Miss Ethel's sister!" Then Rudella crowded in between him and Mr. Jack, and said, "here! get out of my way!" After that she shot arrows at Jimmie Bimm's back till he grew quite nervous.

Piejam is under the desk, eating a banana; he is hiding so he won't have to stop and be introduced to Jimmie Bimm. Zelphina is wondering whether Mr. Jack has brought any candy for her, and if not, she hopes they will go away, so she can play in the room.

When Rudella asked Jimmie Bimm if he were going to stay to dinner, and told him not to sit in her chair, and scolded him for stepping on her arrows, Ethel could stand it no longer and said:

"Rudella, I don't know *what* Mr. Bimm will think of you! You are as rude as a rhinoceros!

Are you a Goop?"

RUDELLA

Rudella, at the Age of Three,
Was Quite as Dear as Dear could Be;
Rudella, at the Age of Four,
Was Not so Charming as Before;
Rudella, at the Age of Five,
Was *Quite* the Rudest Child Alive!

(This Goop is called Rudella because she is so rude)

THIS is Stinjessie's house. It is Number 62 Tulip Street. Stinjessie's room is where the window is, that you just can't see. It is a fine, Spring morning, and Stinjessie has just come out with her things to play on the doorstep. She brought out her doll and her horse and the little table, in her doll's trunk, and then went back for her hoop. Her doll's name is Delia.

Nibolene and Obaynotte are asking Stinjessie if they can play on her doorstep with her toys, and Stinjessie is saying, "no, you can't; I want to play here myself!"

So, when Uncle Harry and Miss Stilcum, of Washington, came down the street, Nibolene and Obaynotte went along with them.

After they had left, Stinjessie was sorry she had not let them stay, for now she had to play all the forenoon alone. So, after she had taken her doll's clothes out of the trunk and dressed her, she said, "Delia, I hope you won't grow up to be as selfish and stingy as your mother, but I am *afraid* you are getting more like me every day!

Are you a Goop?"

STINJESSIE

Stinjessie!—What a Darling Dear!
How Well she used to Persevere!
How Well she Cared for all her Frocks
And Put Away her Building Blocks!
But Would she Let her Playmates Touch
A Toy of Hers?   No, *Sir!*   Not *Much!*

(This Goop is called Stinjessie because she is so stingy
with her toys and things)

TEEZA and KRYSOE have been making a little village in their sand heap, behind the barn. Miss Curleykew has told them that they must stay inside the fence. She is playing tennis with Cousin Billy.

"*Please* can't we go out and get some stones!" Teeza is saying.

"I told you that you must stay in," Miss Curleykew is saying.

"But we *need* the stones, for our wall! It isn't strong enough without them!" Teeza teased.

Miss Curleykew only said, "Love, Thirty!"

for she wanted to go on with her game.

"*Please* can't we?" Teeza said again.

"No, dear," said Miss Curleykew, and then she ran for the ball.

Verivaine was so intent upon looking at herself in her mirror that she walked right into the tennis court, and Miss Curleykew ran into her and knocked her over. But Verivaine was not hurt much.

"Then won't you come and show us how to make a church out of sand?" Teeza said.

"Not now, dear," said Miss Curleykew.

"Why not?" Teeza insisted. "I think it's *mean* you won't come!" Then Cousin Billy shouted, "Teeza, will you tell me something?"

"What is it?" Teeza asked.

"What I want to know is," he said,

"*Are you a Goop?*"

TEEZA

As Bright as Brass, as Good as Gold,
Was little TEEZA, Four Years Old—
Was little TEEZA Mischievous?
Ah No,—she Never Made a Fuss!
But she would Tease to Come or Go
Whenever Mother Told her *"No!"*

(This Goop is called TEEZA because she teases and teases
and teases to do things)

I AM afraid you won't believe
me when I tell you how pert and
saucy and disagreeable Ugpert is.
Think of the worst-behaved child
you know,—Ugpert is worse still. She is not only rude and impolite
to her playmates, but to grown-up people, too.

The Minister has come to call again. Cousin Billy and Miss
Curleykew have been talking to him. Quirita likes the Minister,
because he always gives her a cough-drop when he sees her. She is
eating one now. Goblick has been showing the Minister and Cousin
Billy how well he can snap marbles.

When Ugpert came into the parlor, the Minister said, "how do
you do, little girl, what is your name?"

"Puddin' tame!" said Ugpert, trying to be smart.

"You look as if you had been having a good time," the Minister said.

"You look like a goat!" said Ugpert.

"Oh, Ugpert, how can you *say* such a thing," Miss Curleykew cried.

"I can say it with my mouth!" said Ugpert, trying to be funny.

"Speak politely," said Cousin Billy, "or Dr. White will think
you're a Goop."

"His boots are dirty!" said Ugpert, and she stuck out her tongue
at the Minister and walked off! She *was* a Goop, wasn't she!

Are you a Goop?

UGPERT

Miss UGPERT's Smile was Sweet to See,
For she was Clever as Could Be;
She was not Greedy, Vain or Bad,
Except for One Rude Trick she Had
Of Speaking Saucily to Folks,
And Making Pert Remarks and Jokes.

(This Goop is called UGPERT because she is ugsome
and pert)

ETHEL is going to be married in a week, and the dressmaker is finishing the last of her dresses. Just now, she is hanging a drop skirt and pinning it even, all round. Verivaine has been watching the dressmaker, wishing that she could have some new frocks made, for she loves to dress up and show herself off.

Verivaine thinks she is so pretty that she spends half her time in front of the mirror, nodding her head this way and that, and prinking like a cockatoo. She has been looking in Ethel's bureau drawers and has taken out and tried on all Ethel's jewelry. She put on three rings and two necklaces and four diamond pins and then went and sat by the window, so that people could see her. She has arranged her veil a different way over her head and she thinks she is very beautiful.

A favorite trick of hers is to walk slowly up and down the steps of the finest house in the neighborhood, so that people will think she lives there. Did you ever hear of anyone as vain as that?

Destroya is letting the dressmaker use her scissors, but wants to use them

herself in a minute, to cut the picture of a horse out of the newspaper. Surleigh is saying, "Oh, I see a mouse!" hoping Ethel will jump up on a chair. But Ethel does n't believe him.

When Ethel turned round, she laughed to see Verivaine still before the mirror. "Oh, Verivaine, there's a Goop in the glass!" she said,

"Are you a Goop?"

VERIVAINE

I Think of VERIVAINE as One
So Pretty, and so Full of Fun,
That I would Walk a Mile or Two
To Call upon her.   Would n't You?
But if you Called, I Fear, Alas,
You'd Find her Prinking at the Glass!

(This Goop is called VERIVAINE because she is so very
vain that she spends too much time before the mirror)

MR. JACK and Ethel have already begun to receive their wedding presents, and they are opening them, and making a list of them. Wonty and Whynotte are helping them. When the front door bell rings, both the twins rush downstairs and take the parcels and bring them up to Ethel. Whynotte is wearing one of Wonty's dresses.

After they had done this a while, the twins wanted to open the packages themselves. Wonty opened one, and found a bust of Shakespeare from Mr. Snale, and Whynotte opened another and found a picture of the Minister which he had sent himself. But after they had opened a few more, they got the cards all mixed up, so that Ethel could not tell who had sent the presents. Wonty put Cousin Billy's card on a satin-lined brush and comb case, that looked like a book when it was shut.

Mr. Jack thought it must be one of Billy's jokes. But it was really Mary the maid who had sent it. Whynotte put Miss Stilcum's card on a clock that Prof. Inchworm had sent.

Then Ethel said, "you must not open any more parcels!" and Whynotte said, "Why not?" She began to open another.

Then Mr. Jack said, "you must leave all the presents alone!" and Wonty said, "I won't!" And she kept on touching them.

That is the way they *always* behaved. They usually kept right on as they were doing before. They were Goops, and couldn't help it.

Are you a Goop?

WONTY & WHYNOTTE

WONTY and WHYNOTTE (they were Twins)
Had Many Virtues, and Two Sins.
So Many Virtues had these Two,
I cannot Tell them All to You.
Their Sins were: That they 'd Disobey
And Whyne in an Unpleasant Way.

(These Goops are called WONTY and WHYNOTTE because
one says " I won't !" when she is asked to do anything and the other says " Why not ?" when
her mother refuses to let her do anything)

XCITABELLE has been excited all day. She gets excited very easily, and screams and makes a great noise and rushes about like mad whenever anything happens. To-day she is giving a party. When she was in Kindergarten she got up and ran up to her teacher many times and shouted out, "I'm going to have a party to-day!" till she had to sit all alone till she could grow quiet.

In the afternoon she could hardly wait till she was dressed, but kept jumping up and down and running up and down stairs like a runaway horse. When Cousin Billy came, she ran to meet him with a loud scream, and then ran upstairs shouting at the top of her voice, "COUSIN BILLY'S COME!" She slammed the doors and tipped over chairs until Mother told her she would have to be sent to bed if she did n't act more quietly.

Now they are having the party, and Cousin Billy is playing "Blind Man's Buff" with them. Xcitabelle is shrieking and laughing at the top of her voice, and hopping up and down and stamping her feet, she is having such a good time. No one can be so noisy as Xcitabelle, when she is playing a game, not even Yellkum.

When they had finished the game, Xcitabelle ran all over the house crying, "WE'RE GOING TO HAVE ICE-CREAM! WE'RE GOING TO HAVE ICE-CREAM!"

Then Cousin Billy said, "Yes, Mary is setting the table and there will be ice-cream; but it is not for Goops!

Are you a Goop?"

XCITABELLE

Xᴄɪᴛᴀʙᴇʟʟᴇ when Calm and Mild
Was Simply Perfect, (for a Child)
You'd Want to Hug her Where she Stood,
She was so Quiet and so Good!
But when she Got Excited—*Well!*
You *Ought* to See her Jump and Yell!

(This Goop is called Xᴄɪᴛᴀʙᴇʟʟᴇ because she is so
excitable that when she plays she shrieks
and behaves roughly)

YUWANDA was forbidden ever to go outside the front gate, but this morning she waited till no one was looking, and ran down the road. She found Whymusty playing on some lumber in front of Mr. Jack's new house. He pulled a board off the top, put it across a saw-horse to make a see-saw, and asked Yuwanda to tilt with him. The man sitting on the fence is a carpenter.

While Yuwanda was up high in the air, Why-musty saw a policeman coming along. Why-musty was afraid of being scolded for meddling with the boards, so he started to get off and run away. The policeman came up just in time to save Yuwanda from a bad fall, and he scolded Whymusty for being so thoughtless.

Mary the maid is running to get Yuwanda, for Father has just come home and wants to take her to Boston with him on the next train. Father and Mother are both calling her.

But Yuwanda was so late that she could n't be dressed in time. Father was angry and said, "you disobeyed me, so now you will have to stay at home with Mary.

Are you a Goop?"

YUWANDA

Yuwanda had the Kind of Looks
You Read About in Fairy Books!
She was as Sweet as she was Fair,
So she was Welcome, Everywhere.
And Therefore, Everywhere she *Went* —
Nor Stopped to Ask her Ma's Consent!

(This Goop is called Yuwanda because she runs away
and wanders off to places without asking permission)

THIS is Ethel's wedding, and she is walking up the aisle with her father. Poutine is the flower-maid and is strewing roses on the floor. Lemeetri is carrying the ring on a cushion. Rudella and Carolesse are holding the bridal veil. All the Goops are there, and they have left their toys in the vestibule. Mr. Jack's twin brother is on one of the front seats.

Zelphina was to have been flower-maid, and this is how it happened that she is not. She kept Mary the maid busy waiting on her, and let all the others dress themselves as best they could. When she was all ready, her mother asked her to help Fijetta get her shoes on. But as Zelphina wanted to see which carriage she was going in, she ran away instead, and hid in the pantry where her mother could n't find her. There she stayed, watching out the window.

While she was there, it came time for Ethel to go to the church, and as no one could find Zelphina, Poutine was asked to take her place as flower-girl. When Zelphina came out, all the family had driven off without her. So she had to walk to church and sit all alone. That is what came of her being so selfish a Goop.

Are you a Goop?

ZELPHINA

ZELPHINA Actually Thought
She Did Precisely as she Ought;
She did not Disobey One Rule
That she was Taught at Home or School;
But More than This is Necessary,
ZELPHINA, she was Selfish, *Very!*

(This Goop is called ZELPHINA because she thinks only
of herself and what she wants to do)

ENDING:

Thus I must finish, for the present,
My catalogue of Goops unpleasant;
For, though there may be many more
Who tease, exasperate, or bore,
I cannot recollect the rest,
Though I have done my very best.
Look in the glass and you will see
A different kind of Goop, maybe!
If there are new ones that you know,
I hope that you will tell me so!

Gelett Burgess